A Taste of Blood

A Collection of Vampire Poetry and Short Stories

by T.J. Brown

ISBN: 978-0-557-49488-0
Copyright @ Timothy Brown
May 29, 2010

the kiss of death

Tears of blood this demon cries,
from its dark and soulless eyes.
the night brings only pain,
and life extended from ill gain.
corpses litter the basement floor,
bodies that shall breath no more.
Damnation and eternal night ,
born to a world devoid of light.
savage hunger lies within,
my life itself a mortal sin.
I am a beast without a sire,
born in hell from its great fire.
smell the brimstone on my breath,
I bring with me the kiss of death.
I crave the blood and supple flesh,
so wet and red and fresh.
I feel it running down my chin,
aroused as I commit such sin.
savagely I rape your flesh
and sup your soul through blood still fresh.
I am a creature of the dark,
a heart that beats but holds no spark.
no warmth no love only dreams of flesh and blood.
I have no wants only needs
the ones my sick desire breeds.
So heed my words and know this well;
beware the the dark and do not dwell.
ill suck your soul and send your corpse to hell.

Bitten

Bitten by infatuation stalked in my dreams
pursued by a beauty like none I've never seen.
oh the feeling of love that radiates from her,
it makes me happier then Ive ever been before.
then I awake to find it was no more then a dream.
sadness takes me over and depression;
it squeezes me like a vice to be teased in such manner
with happiness like I have never known or ever will.
the bottle it sooth's me but not tonight; no not tonight.
this time the pain is to much to bare,
I can take it no longer.
And as my depression peaks its highest, a vision appears.
the gun slips from my hand to the floor,
I am staring at a vision almost to beautiful to behold.
her skin pale like marble and her hair like crimson fire.
I am breathless with awe and amazement
as she stares upon me.
Her voice like music from heaven as she spoke to me.
“no my love I will not lose you again.
I have loved you always.
I have waited for you for a very long time,
your sadness is over
for I am here now and shall always be.”
she extends her arms and takes my hands in hers,
pulling me off the floor where I sit.
she says, “come to me,”
her open arms so welcoming as she embraces me.
a kiss upon my forehead, a kiss upon my cheek.

she says, “you will never be sad again i will see to it.”
Then her body made me feel everything
that I had felt in her words,
and as the first rays of light filtered through the curtains
she says, “sleep now my love and fear no more,
for we shall be together always
and i knew true happiness.”
As I drifted off to sleep,
I knew I would never be sad again.
then I opened my eyes fearing it was all a dream;
but there she was smiling upon me,
her hand caressing my face.
I moved to kiss her,
but stopped short with a pain in my neck,
thinking I must have slept wrong, I rubbed it for a second
and to my surprise I found two large bites in my neck.
Mystified, I stared at her as she giggled.
“I'm sorry,” she says,
“but I did say we would be together always.”
Then as she smiles, I see them: two long, ivory-like fangs!
Shocked, but yet I had no fear!
Her love was genuine,
of that I was absolutely sure,
And to be honest, what did it matter?
If I was happy; and I was happier then I have ever been.
As if she could read my thoughts, she smiled and said,
“Good. Now kiss me, I do so love kissing you,
but I should warn you,” and laughing says,
“I probably should have warned you sooner,
I leave bite marks .!”

The Unholy

Defied by the light, condemned to darkness;
I walk this world alone and hungry.
Controlled by a thirst,
a craving that will not be denied.
My legend is a living nightmare,
to gaze upon me is to gaze upon the face of death.
You shall deny me nothing just look into my eyes,
ablaze with the fires of damnation look and behold,
for you will see an unholy power like no other.
touch my flesh and feel the cold of death upon
your finger tips,
as chills of fear ripple down your spine,
and know that its to late, you are now mine.
smell the ghastly reek of my breath,
heavy with the odor of old blood,
and know the evil that walks the night,
an evil as old as creation,
a creature enslaved by darkness,
and his own unholy thirst for blood.
time is his only enemy, for time is all he has left.
so old now,
that killing and death are all he truly remembers.
Forgetting only when he drifts off into a dreamless sleep,
as the sun starts to rise once again,
waiting for the darkness,
so he can once again feed his thirst,
and extend his decrepit,
loathsome life the life of the unholy.

Immortality's lies

The sun shall set, the moon shall rise.
fire burns inside my eyes.
death shall come, for its all i bring,
not quite human,
an immortal thing.
Hatred burns deep inside.
there is no paradise,
just immortality's lies.
the loneliest creature
there will ever be,
alone for all eternity.
Feeding on blood
in the dead of the night.
a heart of darkness
craving the light,
living dreamless days
and tortured nights.
Praying for a death
that he will never find.
wanting the life
that he left behind.
Eternally dammed,
he fell for the lies.
now bloody tears
will he eternally cry,
a vampire, and a victim
of immortality's lies.

Those Who Hunt The Night

The darkness brings forth the hunger,
and those who hunt the night.
It brings forth dangers
the mortal mind could never comprehend.
A creature who's will to live is so strong
he will survive by any means,
feeding off the life of others.
Stalking the darkness which he calls home.
His powers overwhelming,
his eyes alone can render a person powerless,
breaking your will and making it his own.
To look deep into his eyes
is to see a glimpse of hell.
For there is nothing there
but pain torment and death.
He is a soulless creature a beast
who knows nothing of love only death;
who knows only loneliness
and nothing of companionship;
who knows only darkness and hunger.
He will never know the joys of love or companionship.
His immortal life empty,
his immortality a curse upon mankind
as well as himself.
It's sad really,
that he will never know peace or love,
and happiness will never enter his black heart.
He was doomed from the start,

his immortality was not a gift,
it was a curse.
A Pandora's box,
a private hell he calls immortality.
Everything has a price,
but for him the price was to high.
It cost him his mortality,
and his soul.

An Immortal Hate

The darkness brings danger and hate, and resentment.
Hate for the thing that i am,
A parasite that feeds off of the blood of mortals.
Resentment for what you are,
for you being what i want to be,
for the life you possess, the mortality.
Every night as i feed, i feel the hatred!
Hatred for the one thing you possess
that i can never have,
so i feast upon thy life with joy and lust.
My resentment strong;
Who are you, to have what i can not?
When i have all the powers of darkness
at my very command.
I kill to satisfy my thirst
and my hatred for you,
you who are beneath me,
yet are so much more then I.
So i feed, and i kill, and i kill again.
my hate so strong,
because i possess immortality,
but you possess a soul.

The Infinite Ones

The infinite ones, the immortals;
Savage creatures with hungry eyes
and fangs like a beast of destruction
and an appetite for blood,
leaving only death in their wake.
Eyes like fire and a soul as black as night,
Seduction, a weapon for them.
Love is an incomprehensible notion.
Their only emotions are hunger and lust.
Feeding off the blood of others,
thriving off our fear and terror
at the mere site of their immortal eyes,
they offer deceptions and half truths,
seducing us with offers of eternal life.
But its lies,
half truths that we will regret very quickly,
if we give in, and if we don't, we die.
We become a meal to these infinite beasts.
We should fear the things that go bump in the night.
We should fear the darkness,
for there are dangers in it
beyond our wildest imaginations.
Things that kill;
we are prey.
There is evil in the darkness,
and it is coming.

The Lord Vampire

Run screaming into the night,
but i shall find you.
Your clothes shall be torn away
like your inhibitions,
and the blood shall flow from your neck,
as you feed me.
Then the desire, you will give yourself to me.
My will be done, you shall tremble and quake in my thrall.
You shall scream with the force of my passion.
I shall penetrate you to the deepest part of your being,
Your flesh burning at my touch, like velvet fire;
scorching an searing you as I penetrate to your very soul,
you shall be mine for eternity;
A mistress of the night to quench my dark desires.
I am the evil, that is darkness i am;
The Lord Vampire.
Mortals are my play things,
they give me such a thrill.
But i get bored so easily,
and that is when i kill,
I rule the night with evil.
I rule with sheer desire.
I am the master of the night.
Your evil Lord vampire.
So, quench my thirst,
appease my lust; and fulfill my sick desires.
And spend an eternity of darkness
with the Lord of all vampires.

She Belongs to the Night

The darkness takes over the light,
squeezing the essence of everything human.
This is my time, it will be our time.
Are you ready, My Lady?
        Yes, master. Is it time?
Yes My Lady, it is time to begin.
        Will it hurt master?
No, My Lady, but it will change you.
        Master?
Yes, My Lady?
        Will I like it?
Yes, My Lady, you will.
The darkness will take over,
it will change you.
You will be new, better.
You will be one with the darkness,
the night will be ours.
You shall be my queen, my queen of the night.
The darkness shall be your home,
it will comfort you and keep you safe.
Are you ready now, My Lady?
        Yes, Master, I am.
Then we shall begin your new life now.
Tilting her head to the side,
I bite deep into her neck,
The blood flows freely into me.
Her new life begins now,
no longer will she be lonely,

or sick, or frail.
To never know fear again,
for now she belongs to me;
she belongs to the night.

The Companion

He stalks her, watching her through her window
from the darkness.
He has done this for a while now,
she fascinates him;
she is so very like him, tormented and lonely.
He has been thinking about taking her,
changing her; but he is unsure,
tonight will be the night though;
one way or the other.
She will feed him, join him, or die;
but he will give her something that he never had;
a choice.
Yes, he has made up his mind.
She will have a choice.
He enters while she sleeps, but does she sleep?
No, he hears her soft weeping, then she stirs.
She turns to face him as if she senses his presence.
His eyes, like holes, falling into endless sleep.
They offer so much; yet there is a darkness.
One... she longs for... yet fears.
His eyes glow like fire, and she shivers.
She stares at him as if mesmerized, entranced.
Her skin is hot from sleep,
And his voice is like velvet
running along her body.
He speaks and she cowers;
he says "I am the taker of life,
and the giver of death.

I am the holder of immortality,
the lord of the night.
I am all things feared,
you may feed me, and be a slave to my thirst;
you may ask me to end this pathetic existence,
or shall live through the night by my side
and end your loneliness and mine.
You may be the blood that keeps me alive,
or you may rule the night beside me
and be the love that makes me crave life once more.
Or you may have the death
that you have been asking for, for so long.
She shivers at his voice and the thoughts it brings.
Can it really be true?
Can i finally have what I longed for, for so long?
What do I do? Which should i pick?
His offer; fearsome, and yet entrancing.
Take me, do with me as you will,
Anything is better then this life that I must live.
She sits up, the covers falling from her body.
Hesitating slightly,
Wondering, 'did i make the right choice?'
She pulls her hair to the side,
exposing her slender white neck.
She has made her choice and he is happy,
and she is finally at peace;
feeling his fangs welcoming trespassing upon her.
Finally another like himself,
with which to share the night.
To end his loneliness once and for all;
Immortality just got a little better.

The Craving

I crave the blood of others.
When darkness falls,
my wings spread and I fly.
Darkness embraces me like no other,
the tender caress of a lover lost.
The beast wants control.
Tired of the weakness of thought,
it wants pure instinct;
the savage set free.
Evil and decadence always, no escape.
The crimson river flows,
death the only thing I sire.
Life is a dream form which you will awake unto me,
you will awake unto death: undeath, torture.
To awake in the darkness of me;
to awaken in hell,
for hell hath no fury like me.
The eternal fire of damnation
starts right here with me.
One bite shall destroy;
salvation lost.
Everyone has their own hell.
You found yours, when you looked into my eyes.
Say your prayers,
say all your goodbyes.
Then look at me
and prepare to die.

A Love Undying

My love taken from me on the very night
of my unholy union with the darkness,
but never lost, my love for her thrives.
The only sunlight i see now,
is in the memory of her eyes.
She was my only light in this dark life;
but still, hope carries me onward,
for her soul shall live once again,
and i shall once again find her.
My love returned, once again shall my darkness
be filled with light and sunshine.
My world complete once more.
Constantly I search, for I can feel her once again;
once more is she within my grasp.
Longing to hold her once more.
The mere thought can bring me to tears of joy.
Even this unholy darkness of my curse
can not keep out the light of her love,
or the warm fire that burns in my cold heart.
Cursed I may be, but blessed am I,
for I have once, and shall again, feel her love.
Am I a soulless creature of darkness?
No, for she is my soul!
And to once again hold her love
is all the heaven i will ever need.
Maybe I am not cursed after all,
for although my love has died,
we are blessed with a love undying.

The Food Of The Gods

In the hours of dusk between day and night,
before the darkness takes over,
something stirs in the night.
A creature;
Awakened and hungry he rises,
the scent of death clinging to him,
decay surrounds him,
from the rotting remains of his evil hunger,
his victims,
rotting shells of what used to be human beings.
Innocents; victims of an uncontrollable lust for blood.
An evil as ancient as time,
he stalks, he kills, he feeds; this is his life.
He does not age.
He shall never know the ravages of time.
Intelligent, cunning, seductive, and charming,
Thinking himself as a god.
For who else can live eternal, never growing old,
with no fear of death?
Who but a god can sustain life from blood,
and who but a god could give a mere mortal immortality?
He know who fears him.
He can smell your blood,
and he wants it; he needs it,
and will take it from you.
Your faith will not protect you,
for in the darkness, he is lord and master.
When the darkness swallows the light,

he shall hunt, his need to feed is great.
His lust is all consuming.
He shall search out his victims.
Will you be one?
I fear you will, so beware!
Stray not into the darkness,
for evil awaits, and it is hungry.
Those who walk the night,
may become the food of the gods.

The Precious Gift of LordVampirEternal

Out of the darkness I come,
springing forth from the shadows.
My heart a living darkness set inside a body,
a body that hungers and craves,
that feeds upon the blood,
that takes pleasure from flesh.
Do not stray forth into the night,
for it is my home.
Trespass not into the darkness, for many lose their way.
It puts your life, and your very soul at risk.
Many stray into the darkness
seeking my sweet gift of immortality.
But it is a precious gift,
and many find only terror and death.
Why do so many seek my gift?
Is the risk truly worth the reward?
So few are worthy of such a gift,
and so few ever survive,
some become food for my eternal hunger.
Some may serve me.
Some even survive, only because they amuse me.
While others, others please me
with their soft, supple flesh,
servicing my needs with their bodies;
creating a heat within this cold existence.
So few receive my most precious gift,
and i await the day I find the one!
The one who truly deserves my gift.

A true companion,
someone to end an eternity of loneliness,
with which to share my powers;
my secrets, my darkness,
and my cold, unnatural life.
When I find her, can she warm this cold heart?
I know not.
Can she bring back the joy I once had?
I know not.
Can she once again make me feel love?
Again i know not,
but i await.
Eagerly, i wait, and i hope beyond all hope
that she can do just that.
That she can bring back some life
to this unnatural life of mine;
to bring some love, and maybe,
a little piece of mortality back to me.

LordVampirEternal

Blood of Innocents

I feast with decadence upon mortality's flesh,
taking sustenance from the blood of innocents.
Weep not, that the night comes,
but take heed, for with the darkness I arise;
shaking off the dust of this dank
and musty tomb in which i rest.
Filling the night with evil and death,
the stench of my decaying soul
implanting fear in the hearts of my victims.
They shiver in my presence,
for I am death embodied;
the ultimate hunter,
Thee nocturnal beast of prey.
I am an abomination to all that is holy;
an unnatural creature
with the power to not only bring death,
but to grant eternal life.
I am a lord eternal;
Mine is the blood of life.
The night is Mine to rule, and rule I shall.
Humans nothing more then play things,
a source of food to extend my unholy life.
I am thee one true evil.
I feel no remorse, nor love.
No guilt have I,
For I have embraced the darkness
and the creature I have become,
just as all those i create shall come to embrace it.

When I come for you,
will you embrace death,
Or shall you beg for your pathetic life?
I guess we shall see soon,
For...
I am coming...

The Song of The Night

As power beats through my ancient heart,
the night immortal sings to me a melody of time.
A song of birth and death,
of immortality's delights and a terrible inner longing
that is my dark and lonely life.
Blood drips from the lyrics
as the night, it calls my name
and I arise once more,
so I may feast again,
so I may know another night.
Another century of loneliness
extending what little life I have,
So that I may know constant sorrow
and cause countless heartache,
never knowing peace.
Infinite sadness is all I know.
Death is all I bring
to all those who cross my path.
Its a deviant song, the song of the night,
and its the only song I know.
Its rhythm is madness,
its melody tormenting,
but it sings on, and it sings only to me.
As a shadow crosses over my face,
and my hunger grows,
so does my sorrow.
Time is my enemy,
for it is all I have,

its all I know.
I know the pain I cause,
but can anyone see my pain?
Is it written upon my face?
Is the loneliness there?
Is the regret, or the longing,
or is it hidden behind my immortal eyes?
Or behind my darkened heart?
What is life without joy,
without love or companionship?
It is my life, my very existence.
It is all I have;
that, and my tormenting song.
A song of immortality,
the song of the night.

Children of The Night

Where be thy children of the night, but in the darkness.
Thy creatures that thrive on blood for life,
that use lust and arousal as a weapon
with hypnotic eyes, and a mesmerizing gaze.
Where be thy hunters, but stalking their pray?
And where lays thy tomb, where thou does rest,
but in a dark decrepit place
dank with decay and the scent of blood,
where common mortals fear to tread.
Where rest thy dreams, but in a coffin at daybreak.
And where resides our soul,
but in the dark recesses of hell.
Where cometh our strength but from immortality,
and from where forth do we come,
but from the blackness in which we dwell.
From the recesses of the darkness we emerge,
coming forth to feast and ravage;
to control and manipulate,
to devour and consume,
and to create.
To create more children of the night
to fill the darkness with our kind.
To hunger for the blood of thy mere mortals,
and to savagely take sin upon their supple flesh.
We shall dominate and desecrate all mankind,
fore we are the ancients.
We are superior.
We are thy power in the night.

So, where forth does thy death come from?
Look into my eyes,
for your death shall come from me,
and from you shall come my eternal life.
So, where forth lies the fear in the night,
but from thy children of the night.

A Feast of Blood

Discontent follows me from my slumber
like the darkness follows the sun,
waiting to swallow it;
to cast the world into blackness.
I can hear the blood pumping through mortal veins.
I can smell their nearness,
I close my eyes,
following their scents
to see a picture with senses beyond sight.
I see something.
"Oh yessss... I see supple white skin.
I see full robust bodies,
tonight I shall feast.
Oh how times have changed.
From castles to condo's,
no one believes anymore,
until they are looking into my eyes,
but the blood is the same, sweeter perhaps,
for mortals today are so much more full of life.
Has it really been three hundred years?
My how time does fly,
so many places and so many names,
so much blood.
The blood is life, you know.
It is the essence upon which I feast.
It satisfies my hunger, and sustains my life.
Three hundred years of blood, and sins of flesh,
and no end in sight.

I love the life I have.
It's an obscenity in, and of, itself;
full of lust, depravity, passion,
and the darkest of desires;
It is eternally long, but it is mine,
and I cherish it so.
So I shall continue it.
Feasting upon blood,
committing sins upon flesh,
and acts of utter depravity.
So, I eagerly await more feasting and sin,
meeting in the dark of night,
to another three centuries,
so you better start believing,
because I will come for you.
Vampires do exist,
and our life is a feast of blood!"

The Evil of the Night

Carried to me on the wind is a scent.
It is flesh and blood.
Licking my lips at the thought
of that sweet red nectar.
Tasting the air,
intoxicated by the aroma.
My breath coming faster now,
my mind spins with wild thoughts.
Excitement fills me,
courses through my veins.
The next breeze brings another scent,
the aroma of womanhood,
my excitement increases,
the pleasures of blood and flesh await me.
my teeth extend,
lengthening like the razor sharp fangs of a serpent.
The power of immortality coursing through my veins.
I grow erect with arousal,
as I follow the scent I know I must have her.
I shall drink of her blood.
I shall abuse her flesh for my pleasure.
She shall surrender to me,
she has no choice for it is my will.
She will perform upon me sins of such depravity
that she will weep as she does so.
I will enjoy many pleasures in her flesh,
then I shall drink of her blood,
feasting on her fear,

thriving on her terror
and tasting of her soul,
then she shall be broken.
The woman that once was, will be shattered,
nothing but a shell will remain.
But on the next sunset,
from that shell, shall emerge a new woman;
A creature of eternity,
stronger and more cunning,
bold, and with no fear.
She will have a thirst for blood,
and a lusting for all sinful pleasures.
She shall thrive in the darkness,
and never shall she die,
as long as there is blood, there is life.
A companion she shall be,
her full, robust body giving pleasure only to me.
Her will my own, she shall obey only me,
for I am her creator, her god!
For I am death, and I am eternal life.
I am the oldest, living creature that walks the earth.
I am darkness,
I am sin,
I am the evil of the night.
I am a Vampire
]

A Vampires Love

Lusting for the life,
he has not felt for so long,
and all the things he has lost
that will forever be gone,
a vampires love, one eternal kiss.
It's more of a curse
then it is a gift.
Thirsting for blood,
prolonging a life
that's condemned him only
into eternal night.
Sadness it plagues him,
and longing does ride,
his eternal companion
never leaving his side.
Haunted by specters
of a once normal life,
a home, a family,
and a sweet, loving wife.
Now everything is gone,
all that he had,
and still he lives on.
Eternally sad,
wanting so badly
for all he cant have.
Searching for something
he never will find.
An eternal hell.

In the memories of his mind,
so many things that never again will he know;
like a kiss given with love,
or the soft touch of wife.
For he traded his soul
for this accursed life,
now forever in darkness.
Tears of blood he will cry
as he prays for forgiveness,
so he may die.

The Lord of the Night

When the vampire rises at daylights end,
the blood will flow once again.
Victims will scream, and cry, and beg,
but the blood will flow until they are dead.
Hunger sated, such a thrill,
he enjoys the hunt, the prey, the kill.
Stalking silent, he likes to play
little games with his prey.
Cat and mouse, he likes to chase,
to make them fear,
the terror on their face.
He is the lord of the night,
an unholy power of awesome might.
Gnashing teeth and eyes of fire,
evil as hell is his sick twisted desire.
Dreams of flesh, and rivers of blood,
he has no remorse, no pity, or love.
The night belongs to him, and his sick desires.
Murder and bloodshed are all the he sires.
No mercy or compassion does this creature have.
So if you ever wake in the dead of the night,
to a sudden sound and a terrible sight
of an evil creature who's eyes glow like fire,
then your death is coming,
you have just met a Vampire.

Immortalities Guilt

The night brings bloody tears
and a blood red moon,
sorrow and hate follow me,
sorrow for the humanity Ive lost,
and hate for myself and the creature Ive become.
Blood follows me where ever i go,
I am death,
I fed off of the life of others.
Heart-ache and misery
are all i leave behind me.
Rivers of blood haunt my daytime slumber,
feelings of guilt and remorse haunt my nights,
loneliness haunts my every moment.
Immortality.
I am an accursed creature,
bound by no silly superstitions or fables.
I may walk in the daylight,
but i am much more at home in the darkness,
for it hides me and my shame.
As i walk along my lonely path,
I wonder about my next victim who shall it be.
Maybe it will be you?

One with the Night

I slip into the night silent and unseen.
My vision is sharp and my hearing is keen,
I hunt, for I thirst.
I stalk out my prey, my teeth break flesh.
Life's blood drains away.
I am one with the night,
My eyes glow like fire,
I am the beast you call the Vampire.
I offer you death, you give me life,
I am a creature who is one with the night.
Look into my eyes and become one with the night.
You can not escape me, or my deadly bite.
There's no where to run, and no place to hide,
for I am one with the night,
and I...
        And I will always survive...

The New Life

As I pull into the drive, I wonder...

"has it really been this long, since I have been home?

Almost a decade.

I have stayed away far to long, or haven't I stayed away long enough?"

(sighs)

"I don't know, maybe this was a mistake.

Maybe I should turn around and leave now?

So many bad memories,

all the fighting.

God, it seemed so constant!

It never seemed to stop, that's why I left. I had to leave.

God, look at the house! It has definitely seen better days. It looks like something from a horror film. Guess it's kind of appropriate, my whole life has been a horror, one after another.

I guess I should go in, can't put it off forever. Maybe it will be different with him gone. Maybe. I don't know. It's all crazy.

I mean, I still don't understand how he died. It really doesn't make any sense, how do you die from blood loss with no wounds?

Not that I care, to be honest. I'm glad the bastard is dead.

They called him my father, but he was never a father. He was an angry, evil man who cared for no one.

No one, except himself. If it wasn't for my sister, I wouldn't have even come back.

Upon entering the house, I hear my name screamed excitedly, and i see my sister running to me, giving me long over-due hugs and kisses of welcome. Then, caught completely off guard, she slaps me across the face.

“Damn you! How could you stay away for so long!!! Leaving me here alone with him, just me and mom! How could you?” She sputters in rage.

“How is mom?” He asks, to change the subject and redirect her wrath.

“She is not well. She wont last long,” Her voice heavy with sadness.

“Vicky, I'm sorry, but I couldn't stay. You know I couldn't.” He answers, his own voice heavy with guilt.

“I know, but you must be tired.” She waves him on into the house. “It was a long trip. Why don't you go get some rest, it's late.” She helps bring my luggage inside.

“We can talk more tomorrow, I promise. After all, we have a lot of catching up to do.” Vicky grins, glad her brother is home.

I take the few things I've brought with me to my old room. God, it's like stepping backwards into hell. The memories come rushing back like a slap to the face. Being exhausted, sleep comes quickly, but is restless.

Being here is so strange, it brings back old nightmares, and something else is not right, but I don't know what it is, it's just a eerie, unnatural feeling.

I am startled awake by a scream rending the air. Was that mom? What the hell is going on?

Running into her bedroom, my sister looks up at me

from the edge of mothers bed.

"She is delirious," she says, tears rolling down her cheeks, "it won't be long now, the cancer has devoured her a lot quicker than expected! She wont let me help her. I really can help her, you know! It would be so easy, so quick..."

Her eyes, oh my god, what is wrong with her eyes? How do they glow like that? They are luminescent, like the eyes of some night animal. What in the hell is going on here? My thoughts are broken by a gasp, as my mother takes her final breath.

With a sigh, Vicky rises from the bed. Turning to face me, she smiles. Long, white teeth showing through barely parted lips, teeth like the fangs of a serpent.

"I'm still angry with you, you know, for leaving me here all alone with him," she growls, "but I guess I forgive you too, because with all the terrible things father did to me, he would have done worse but he feared you. He thought you would return and kill him." then she laughs, an evil laugh. "It's really sort of funny, isn't it? He thought it would be you that would kill him. But it was me! I killed him that evil, evil man! And did I ever make him suffer before he died! Just as he made me suffer, but you far worse! The pain he put you through... I hated him for that! I love you, I always have, that will never change! Don't you think I don't know? You thought I wouldn't know how you protected me all those years, Now I want to return the favor. My sweet brother, let me protect you, for a change!"

"Protect me? From what, Vicky? he is long dead. What is there to really protect me from?" I ask her, growing slightly cautious, but more curious than afraid.

"From everything! I want to protect you from everything! Old age, infirmity and death, illness the ravages of time! I want to give you a new life, a life unlike anything you have ever known. A life without fear or guilt. You won't get sick. You won't grow old, and you never, ever die! But, I will not force it upon you, because i love you so. The choice is yours, but i couldn't bare to see you die.

Oh, my God! Vicky! Vicky is a fucking vampire!

As the reality sets in, she approaches. I wonder, 'why don't I run? Why don't I say something to stop her? This is utter madness! It can't be real! It's all happening as if this is a dream; an infernal nightmare! But, what if this is real? Maybe with the life I had, I deserve this! To not grow old, or die. To be strong, not hurt, no pain ever again. Is this my destiny? Is this what I'm fated to become?

Putting her hands upon his face, and gently kissing his lips, she tilts his head.

"This will be the last kiss before your new life begins," She states through ruby lips, a stark contract to her ivory-pale skin, her eyes aglow with deep-rooted emotion. "I do this for you, out of love. Remember that."

Razor sharp canines slide effortlessly into the tender flesh of my neck.

Swooning, the room spinning like the jumble of thoughts in my mind. Filled with a flurry of emotion; love, fear, excitement, all at once. Dizziness sets in and the darkness comes to embrace me.

I shall awake a new, and better man, with a new life. I shall awake a vampire!

As consciousness flees from my grasp, I can see her

face behind closed eyes. I hear her voice, a voice filled with love.

"I have missed you so, dear Brother. But now, we shall make up for lost time. After all, we have all eternity."

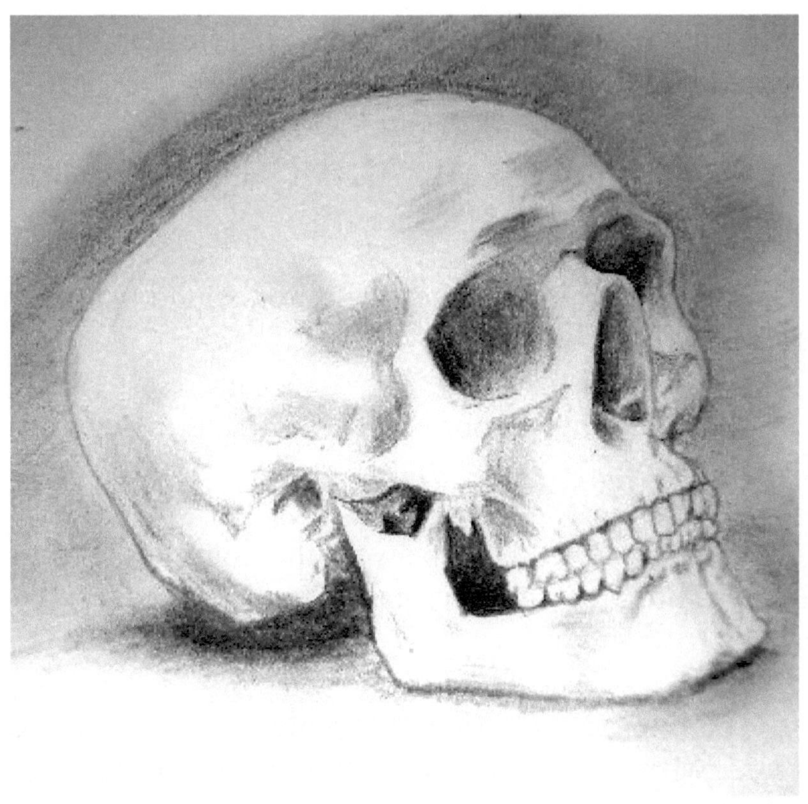

Dedication

A bit of praise here for those of who have been a constant Source of encouragement to me!

First off, my #1 fan supporter, cheerleader, and therapist, Kim Leonard.

My kids who support everything I do, and give me the love to keep fighting.

my good friend, former neighbor, sound board, and editor; Lawrence button.

all those who supported my work and my ego on Allpoetry.com.

To all my friends who swear the novel I intend to write, will not only sell, but make Stephen King tremble in fear.

To all those who tried to trip me up at every turn; It is you, who gave me the drive to see this through. Thanks a bunch.. lol

to my family... who knew nothing about this book but who have been there for me no matter what,

And to my oldest friend Carl L. Just for being you, thanks Bud!!!!!!!!

This book is dedicated to Kaylynn, Jacob, And Renee. Daddy love you.

www.ingramcontent.com/pod-product-compliance
Ingram Content Group UK Ltd.
Pitfield, Milton Keynes, MK11 3LW, UK
UKHW041905190726
13854UKWH00003B/1092